Parents and Caregivers,

Stone Arch Readers are designed to provide enjoyable reading experiences, as well as opportunities to develop vocabulary, literacy skills, and comprehension. Here are a few ways to support your beginning reader:

- Talk with your child about the ideas addressed in the story.

- Discuss each illustration, mentioning the characters, where they are, and what they are doing.

- Read with expression, pointing to each word. You may want to read the whole story through and then revisit parts of the story to ensure that the meanings of words or phrases are understood.

- Talk about why the character did what he or she did and what your child would do in that situation.

- Help your child connect with characters and events in the story.

Remember, reading with your child should be fun, not forced. Each moment spent reading with your child is a priceless investment in his or her literacy life.

Gail Saunders-Smith, Ph.D

STONE ARCH **READERS**

are published by Stone Arch Books
151 Good Counsel Drive, P.O. Box 669
Mankato, Minnesota 56002
www.capstonepub.com

Copyright © 2010 by Stone Arch Books

Library of Congress Cataloging-in-Publication Data
Crow, Melinda Melton.
 Snow trouble / by Melinda Melton Crow ; illustrated by Ronnie Rooney.
 p. cm. — (Stone Arch readers)
 ISBN 978-1-4342-1624-3 (library binding)
 ISBN 978-14342-1755-4 (pbk.)
 [1. Dump trucks—Fiction. 2. Trucks—Fiction.] I. Rooney, Ronnie, ill. II. Title.
PZ7.C88536Sn 2010
[E]—dc22

                                                   2008053407

Summary: Three truck buddies go out for a drive. See which truck ends up sliding
through the snow.

Creative Director: Heather Kindseth
Graphic Designer: Hilary Wacholz

Reading Consultants:
Gail Saunders-Smith, Ph.D
Melinda Melton Crow, M.Ed
Laurie K. Holland, Media Specialist

Printed in the United States of America in Stevens Point, Wisconsin.
032011
006103R

**The little red bird is a friend of the truck pals.
Every time you turn the page, look for it.
Can you find the little bird?**

SNOW TROUBLE

written by
Melinda Melton Crow

illustrated by
Ronnie Rooney

STONE ARCH BOOKS
MINNEAPOLIS   SAN DIEGO

This is Green Truck.
This is Dump Truck.
This is Blue Truck.

Green Truck sees trees.

Dump Truck sees sand.

Blue Truck sees snow.

Oh no! Do you see the ice?

"Oh no!" says Blue Truck.
"I am sliding on the ice."

"Help, help, help!" says Blue Truck.
"Who will stop me?"

Green Truck and Dump Truck
see Blue Truck sliding.

"I will stop you," says
Dump Truck.

Dump Truck gets sand.

"I will stop you too," says
Green Truck.

Green Truck makes a snow pile.
Dump Truck drops the sand.

Blue Truck stops sliding.

"Thank you!" says Blue Truck.
"You are good pals."

STORY WORDS

truck	sand	ice
dump	snow	help
trees	sliding	stop

Total Word Count: 104

Follow your favorite truck pals as they learn about the open road.